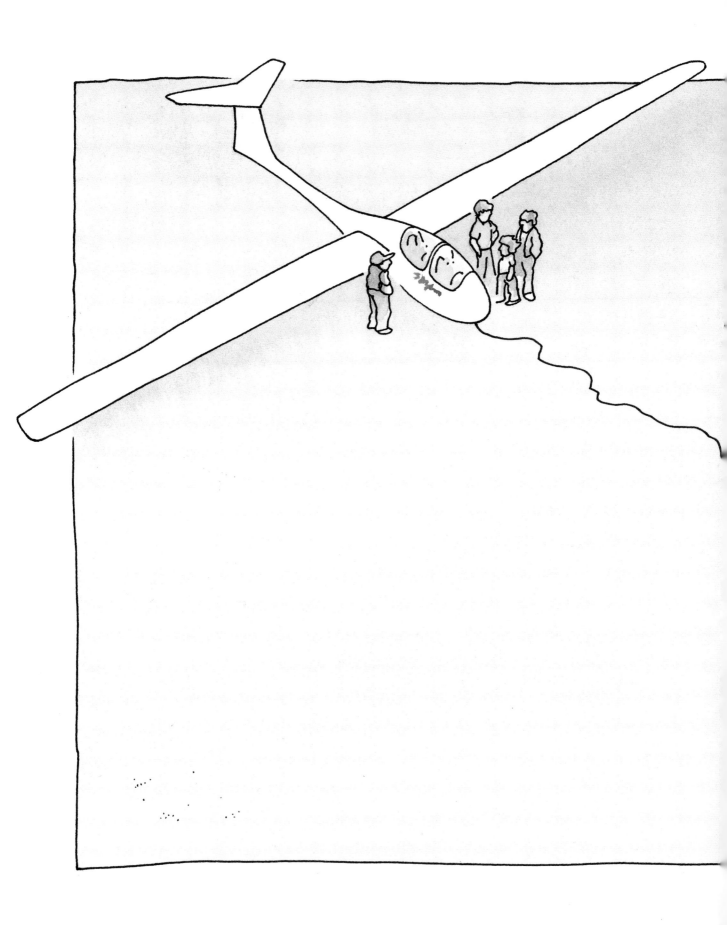

The Sky of Now

by **Chaim Potok**

illustrated by

Tony Auth

Alfred A. Knopf
New York

THIS IS A BORZOI BOOK PUBLISHED BY ALFRED A. KNOPF, INC.

Text copyright © 1995 by Chaim Potok
Illustrations copyright © 1995 by Tony Auth
All rights reserved under International and Pan-American Copyright Conventions.
Published in the United States of America by Alfred A. Knopf, Inc., New York, and
simultaneously in Canada by Random House of Canada Limited, Toronto.
Distributed by Random House, Inc., New York.

Library of Congress Cataloging-in-Publication Data
Potok, Chaim.
The sky of now / by Chaim Potok ; pictures by Tony Auth.
p.   cm.
Summary: A flight lesson aboard Uncle Conor's plane helps ten-year-old Brian
overcome his fear of heights.
ISBN 0-679-86021-5 (trade)
[1. Fear—Fiction. 2. Flight—Fiction.] I. Auth, Tony, ill. II. Title.
PZ7.P8399Sk   1994   93-27540 [E]—dc20

Manufactured in Singapore
10 9 8 7 6 5 4 3 2 1

To pilots and their
passengers everywhere
— C.P.

To Eliza, Katie,
and Emily
— T.A.

The door to Brian's room opened and his mother entered.

"Good morning, Brian," she said. "We want to get an early start."

"I'll get dressed fast," said Brian.

She raised the shades. Brian saw sunlight on the trees and the lawns and houses. A flock of birds flew through the summer sky, their wings barely moving.

After his mother had left, Brian said to Broomer, "We're going to the Statue of Liberty today."

Broomer was the two-foot-high ceramic clown that Uncle Conor, who piloted big jetliners, had sent Brian nearly a year ago from Hong Kong. With the clay clown had come a little book on circuses, and a note. "Dear Brian, Happy ninth birthday! Love, Uncle Conor."

The book explained that the clown performed a balancing act on a wire strung three feet off the ground. In one hand, he carried an umbrella, and in the other, he held a broom. That's why Brian had named him Broomer.

"Are you listening to me?" Brian asked Broomer.

"To every word, kiddo," said Broomer.

"Then please say something," said Brian.

"I hear she's real tall," said Broomer.

After breakfast Brian and his parents and little sister drove into the city. They rode along the Hudson River. Brian felt his heart jump with excitement as they drove past an aircraft carrier.

A little later, Brian's father parked the car. They walked to a dock where people were standing in line.

"That's the Statue of Liberty," said his mother.

Brian looked at the distant statue standing on an island in the middle of the harbor.

"We're going to the top," said his father.

They boarded a ferry. White birds circled the ferry as it moved across the water. Brian watched the statue growing taller and taller.

As they were leaving the ferry, Brian's sister looked at the statue and said, "Are we going *all* the way up?"

"That's right, Jessica," said Brian's mother. "All the way to the top. Isn't it wonderful?"

And up they went, in a crowded elevator, and then up narrow winding stairs into the head of the Statue of Liberty.

Brian made his way to the windows. He had never been this high before. How blue the sky was! He stood up on his tiptoes and leaned forward as far as he could. His nose brushed the window.

Then he looked down.

All at once he felt his heart begin to beat very rapidly. His hands turned cold and sweaty. His knees seemed barely able to hold him.

He looked up at the sky.

He would not look down again. But as soon as he told himself that, he did look down, straight down.

He saw himself slipping through the window and falling.

Down, down, down he fell...

He closed his eyes and stepped back.

Sometime later they took the elevator down.

"How high is the Statue of Liberty?" asked Brian in the car.

"With the base that it stands on, three hundred and five feet and one inch, to be exact," said his father.

"Were you scared up there?" asked his mother.

"A little," said Brian. "But I'm okay now."

The car had barely come to a stop in their driveway when Brian noticed a big wooden crate on the front porch.

Brian's friend Paul came running across the street.

"It's for you, Brian," said Paul. "A man brought it in a truck. I told him you'd be back later, and he left it."

"It's from Uncle Conor," said Brian, looking at the tag on the crate. "Where's Singapore?"

"In Asia," said Brian's mother.

"It's farther away than Hong Kong," said Brian's father. "My brother really gets around, doesn't he?"

"Aren't you going to open it?" asked Paul.

Brian and his father brought tools from the garage. Then Brian helped his father open the crate. There was a lot of paper and plastic inside. Carefully, Brian peeled it all away.

A head appeared, a body, arms, legs.

It was a pilot.

A two-foot-high ceramic figure of a pilot.

Along with the clay pilot was a little book, and a note. "To Brian, A small surprise for your upcoming tenth birthday. Wait'll you see the *big* surprise! Love, Uncle Conor."

The book said that the pilot had flown fighter planes in Europe during the Second World War and shot down seven German aircraft, four over France and three over Germany.

Brian carried the statue of the pilot into his room and put it down next to Broomer.

"I have to give you a name," said Brian.

He thought and thought.

"I'll call you Zoomer," he said, finally. "Because you're a pilot and you go *zooming* through the sky."

"We don't only zoom," said the pilot. "But Zoomer will do fine."

"Hmm," said Broomer.

"I'm tired," said Zoomer. "It's been a long trip."

He seemed to fall asleep.

"He's nice," said Brian.

"You think so?" said Broomer.

"Listen, I had a bad time today," said Brian. "I got real scared of how high I was in the Statue of Liberty."

"Kiddo, anyone with half a brain should be scared of heights," said Broomer.

"How can I be a pilot if I'm scared of heights?" asked Brian.

"You're only nine years old," said Broomer. "Maybe you'll get over it."

The weeks of July went by slowly, and Brian forgot about the Statue of Liberty.

One day in early August, Brian went with his mother to see his father's new office in the Empire State Building.

The ride up reminded Brian of the Statue of Liberty.

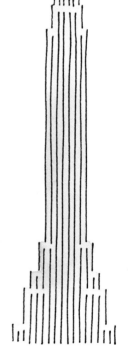

Inside his father's office, while his parents talked together, Brian wandered over to a window and looked out.

He saw the tops of buildings. Without thinking, he rose up as high as he could on his tiptoes and put his nose against the window.

And he looked straight down.

His hands turned icy cold. He could feel his heart beating and his legs trembling.

He saw himself slipping through the window and falling, falling...

He stepped quickly back.

In the elevator on the way down, Brian asked, "How tall is this building?"

"About a thousand feet," said his mother.

"One thousand four hundred seventy-two feet, to be exact," said his father.

The feeling of falling was still very strong inside Brian when he returned home with his parents later that day.

"I was *really* scared this time, " Brian said to Broomer. Broomer smiled sadly.

"Excuse me," said Zoomer. "I couldn't help overhearing. Did you say that you're frightened of heights?"

"I looked out the window of my father's office today and I almost got sick," said Brian.

"When I was about your age," said Zoomer, "I went to Niagara Falls. I stood right near the edge and wondered what it would be like to look down."

"What happened?" asked Brian.

"I decided not to look down," said Zoomer.

The next day Brian asked his friend Paul, "What's the highest place you've ever been?"

"The Grand Canyon," said Paul. "It's about one mile straight down over the edge."

"Were you scared?" asked Brian.

"It was real neat," said Paul. "But my little brother threw up."

 More days went by. A letter arrived for Brian.

"Dear Brian," the letter read. "Just two more weeks until your tenth birthday and the *big surprise*. Love, Uncle Conor."

Brian woke up early on the morning of his tenth birthday. He raised the shades. The sky was blue, with puffy white clouds. Birds glided lazily through the warm summer air.

"Happy birthday, Brian," said his mother when he sat down to breakfast.

After breakfast Brian and his parents and little sister climbed into the car. They rode for a long time on country roads past farms and villages.

Brian felt so excited and curious he couldn't sit still. "Where are we going?" he asked, looking out the car windows at fields and horses and cows.

"If we told you, it wouldn't be a surprise, would it?" said his father.

"It's only a few more miles," said his mother.

"Two point eight miles, to be exact," said his father.

Soon they turned in at a dirt road that led to a group of low buildings and a large grassy field.

Near one of the buildings stood Uncle Conor!

He was talking to an elderly man who wore goggles and an aviator cap with earflaps.

"Happy birthday, Brian!" called Uncle Conor.

Brian ran over, and Uncle Conor gave him a big hug. "I haven't seen you in a long while," said Uncle Conor. "Ready for your surprise?"

Uncle Conor pointed to the edge of the field.

Brian saw a single-engine plane. Behind it was a white aircraft with a very small fuselage and enormous wings. It sat on the ground tilted sideways on one wing.

It had no engine.

Painted in red letters under the cockpit was the name *Skynow*.

"We're going up for a ride," said Uncle Conor.

"We are?" said Brian. His legs were suddenly trembling.

"You want to be a pilot?" asked Uncle Conor.

Brian heard himself say, "Yes."

"Well, you start learning today in this glider," said Uncle Conor.

"Follow me."

He led Brian across the field.

"How high will we be flying?" asked Brian.

"About three thousand feet," said Uncle Conor.

Three thousand feet!

"You sit in the front seat," said Uncle Conor.

Brian climbed into the cockpit and buckled himself into the seat. His father stood near the raised wing. His uncle got into the rear seat and lowered the plastic bubble over their heads.

The man in the aviator cap and goggles climbed into the airplane. The engine sputtered and roared. Brian's father reached up and pulled the glider wing down so it was level with the ground. The plane began to move. And the glider was moving, too, with Brian's father running alongside, keeping the wings level.

Brian realized that the glider was attached by a tow rope to the front plane and was being pulled along.

Uncle Conor sat in the rear seat telling Brian what to expect.

The glider went bumping across the grassy field. Brian saw the airplane leave the ground.

Suddenly the glider was in the air!

Brian curled his toes and took a deep breath. He felt the glider climbing higher and higher.

Up ahead the single-engine plane flew straight on and on, and the tow rope connected to the glider was taut, and below, very far below, were tiny trees and fields.

Brian heard a loud thump, and his heart jumped.

The tow rope had been released.

Brian saw the plane turning away to the left. And the glider was turning right.

What was keeping them from falling?

"The air currents and our long wings," said Uncle Conor, as if he had read Brian's mind.

"The air carries us the way water carries ships."

The air lifted them higher and higher.

Uncle Conor kept on explaining how the glider flew. He was talking about the force of gravity, about what happens when you change direction, about heaviness and lightness. He talked about rising hot air currents called thermals, and how it was natural to feel nervous because of the strange motions and sensations you were experiencing, like sudden bumps and rolling sideways and pitching up and down.

Brian listened, all the time looking up at the sky and hearing the rushing sound of the air through which they were flying.

Then Brian looked down.

He shut his eyes immediately.

The glider climbed and banked and climbed again. Brian kept his eyes tightly closed. They hit a bump and dropped. He felt his stomach moving up toward his throat.

The glider slid sideways in a steep turn, and Brian, telling himself not to open his eyes, opened his eyes.

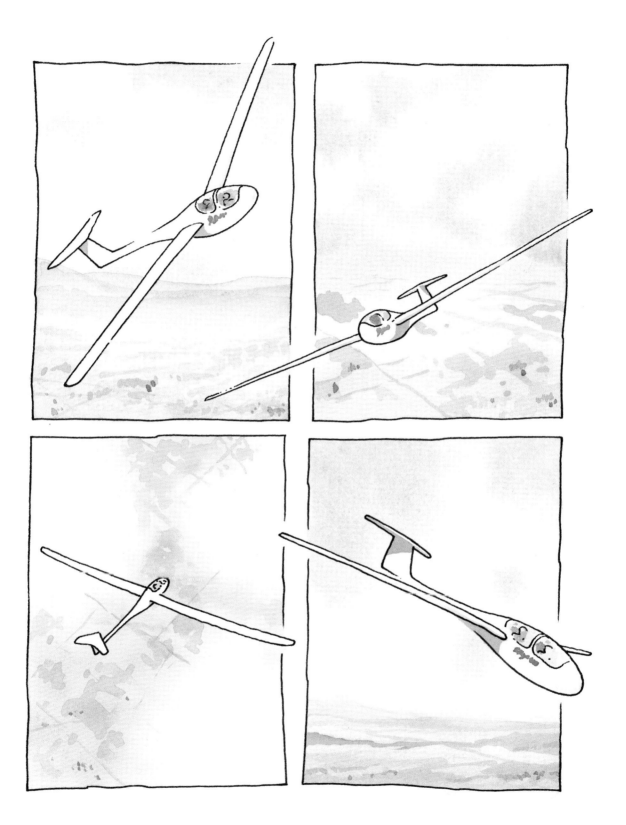

The first thing he saw was that Uncle Conor was not in the pilot's seat.

In the pilot's seat sat—Zoomer!

And next to Zoomer sat Broomer, holding his umbrella and broom.

"Thought I'd take over for a while," said Zoomer. "You don't mind, do you?"

"No," said Brian.

"Reminds me a bit of the war days," said Zoomer.

"What am I doing here?" said Broomer. "This isn't three feet off the ground."

"It's about three thousand feet," said Brian.

"Three *thousand?*" said Broomer. "I never play more than three feet off the ground. Hey, *watch the bumps,* will you?"

"Sorry, old chap," said Zoomer.

"This is *terrible* for my nerves," said Broomer.

"Ready for some *real* surprises?" said Zoomer.

"*Wait* a minute, *wait* a minute," said Broomer. "Let's *talk* about this first."

"Here we go," said Zoomer.

They soared through the blue sky, bouncing on currents of rising air.

All at once they dipped down, and Brian saw streets and houses and lawns—and there was his house and his friend Paul standing on the street, looking up at them. Brian waved to him.

They soared on—over the city and the river.

There was the Statue of Liberty!

Brian saw the window in her head where he had stood a few weeks ago, looking down.

On they flew—past the Empire State Building!

The glider soared, banked, climbed.

Then the city was gone.

Brian saw fields and woods and the bluest of skies.

"Look at *that!*" said Zoomer suddenly.

Brian looked where Zoomer was pointing and caught his breath.

About forty feet away flew a huge bird. Its enormous wings were as straight and still as the wings of the glider.

"It's an eagle!" said Zoomer.

"Now *that's* a surprise!" said Broomer, almost smiling.

Brian sat with his nose pressed to the plastic bubble of the cockpit.

To fly alongside an eagle!

Watching the eagle, its graceful body and huge spread of wings, Brian forgot entirely that he was in an aircraft. He felt the sky opening itself to him, felt himself inside the blueness all around him. He thought only of the sky and the eagle, of this *moment*, this very *special moment* of flying.

He thought only of *now*...

And he laughed with delight and happiness.

"Glad you're having a good time," Brian heard someone say. He turned his head and saw Uncle Conor in the rear seat. They soared on alongside the eagle.

"Beautiful thing to see, isn't it?" said Uncle Conor.

"I was very nervous before," said Brian.

"Anyone who isn't nervous when he first starts flying should have his head examined," said Uncle Conor.

"I'm afraid of heights," said Brian.

"Nearly everyone is afraid of heights," said Uncle Conor. "Fear of heights is very natural, but it has nothing to do with flying."

The eagle flew into a cloud and vanished.

"Time to go home," said Uncle Conor.

They banked steeply.

Brian did not look at the wingtips of the glider but kept his eyes fixed on the nose. Somehow that made it easier to take the turns.

Then he looked down.

That still frightened him—to look straight down that way. But this time he didn't see himself falling.

They flew closer and closer to the ground and then gently set down on the grassy meadow and rolled and came to a stop.

Brian released his seat belt and climbed out of the cockpit. How good the ground felt under his feet!

"You're a fine student," said Uncle Conor.

Brian's parents stood there, smiling.

"I want *my* turn," said Brian's sister.

"Another time, Jessica," said Brian's mother.

"Proud of you," said Brian's father.

Uncle Conor shook Brian's hand. "Happy birthday," he said. "Next year, another flight. Maybe we'll get up to five thousand feet. Or higher. Okay?"

"That'd be great," said Brian.

That night, lying in his bed, Brian said to Zoomer, "Thanks for the ride."

"A pleasure," said Zoomer.

"I was scared," said Brian. "It felt—dangerous."

"Lots of the big things we do have some danger in them," said Zoomer.

"Thanks for coming along," Brian said to Broomer.

"Hey, anything for a friend," said Broomer. "Just don't make a habit of it."

"I'm sleepy," said Brian. "Good night."

"Good night, all," said Zoomer.

Brian had forgotten to lower the shades. Stars shone in a sky of deepest blue—the sky that had earlier carried Brian and his Uncle Conor and the glider *Skynow* and Broomer and Zoomer.

And the eagle.

Lying in his bed and looking out the window at the night sky, Brian saw all of them gliding together, weaving among the stars and soaring up and up and on and on and on...

"Proud of you, Brian," said Broomer. "Good night, kiddo."